C.G.'S CHOCOLATE SALAMI

5 digestive biscuits or favorite cookies, broken into small bits
3 regular-size marshmallows, cut into small pieces
1/4 cup raisins
2-1/2 ounces bittersweet chocolate
2 tablespoons unsalted butter
1 tablespoon heavy (whipping) cream
1 teaspoon honey
confectioner's sugar for dusting

Have ready:
a large piece of plastic wrap

Mix the broken cookies, marshmallows, and raisins in a bowl.

Melt the chocolate, butter, cream, and honey in a microwave for 20 seconds, or in the top of a double boiler. Remove from the heat and stir until the mixture is uniform. If there are lumps, heat a little more. Add the cookie mixture, combining well. Pour the mixture onto the plastic wrap. Press and squeeze into a salami shape, then wrap it tightly. Refrigerate for at least 6 hours.

Remove the plastic wrap from the "salami," dust with confectioner's sugar, and cut into thin slices. Oo la la! Delicious!

C.G.'S BERRY PETIT CREAM CHEESE TARTS

2 whole graham crackers
1/2 cup cream cheese
2 tablespoons heavy (whipping) cream
2 tablespoons honey
1 cup fresh raspberries or other favorite berries

Have ready:
4 ramekins or custard cups

Crush the graham crackers. Divide the crumbs evenly among the ramekins. In a medium bowl, whisk the cream cheese, cream, and honey until thick and creamy. Spoon over the graham cracker crumbs. Arrange the berries on top. Chill. Serve within 2 hours after preparing. Bon appétit!

For Jakub, Ana, and Hanoch, who are always
looking for something to nibble.

Special thanks to Jordi and Pilar.

Published by Schwartz & Wade Books, an imprint of Random House Children's Books, a division of Random House, Inc., New York
Copyright © 2009 by Janet Stein
All rights reserved.
Schwartz & Wade Books and colophon are trademarks of Random House, Inc.

Visit us on the Web! www.randomhouse.com/kids
Educators and librarians, for a variety of teaching tools, visit us at www.randomhouse.com/teachers

Library of Congress Cataloging-in-Publication Data
Stein, Janet (Janet Lenore).
This little bunny can bake / Janet Stein. — 1st ed.
p. cm.
Summary: Animals come from far and wide to study at the world-famous dessert school of Chef George.
ISBN 978-0-375-84313-6 (trade) — ISBN 978-0-375-95413-9 (glb)
[1. Baking—Fiction. 2. Desserts—Fiction. 3. Rabbits—Fiction. 4. Animals—Fiction.] I. Title.
PZ7.S82145Th 2009
[E]—dc22
2008005866

The text of this book is set in Stempel Schneidler. ✳ The illustrations are rendered in brush and ink. ✳ Book design by Rachael Cole.

PRINTED IN CHINA
10 9 8 7 6 5 4 3 2 1
First Edition

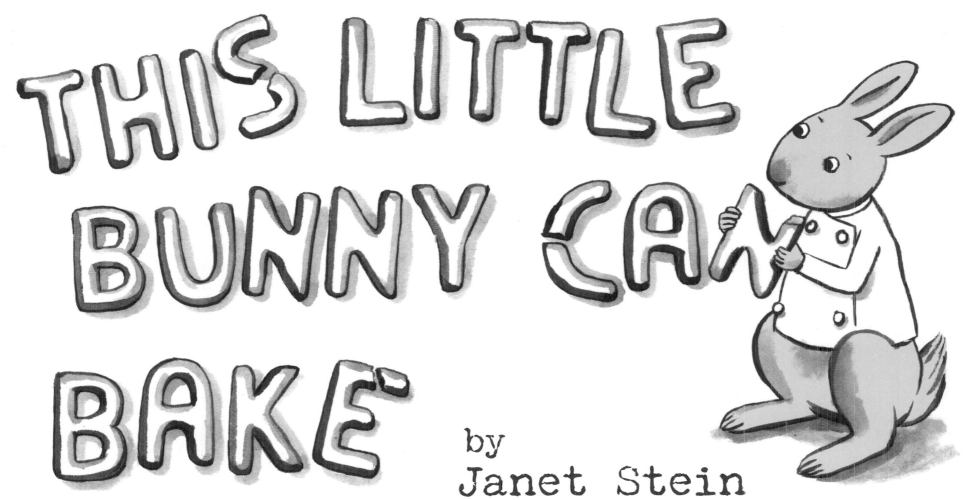

THIS LITTLE BUNNY CAN BAKE

by
Janet Stein

schwartz & wade books · new york

Hurry, class is about to begin!
Following their noses, the new students arrive one
by one at Chef George's world-famous dessert school.

Eager students have come from far and wide to study with the master pastry chef.

"*Bonjour*, everyone. I am Chef George. I know everything there is to know about dessert. And as of now, you know absolutely nothing! But I will teach you. It's very simple."

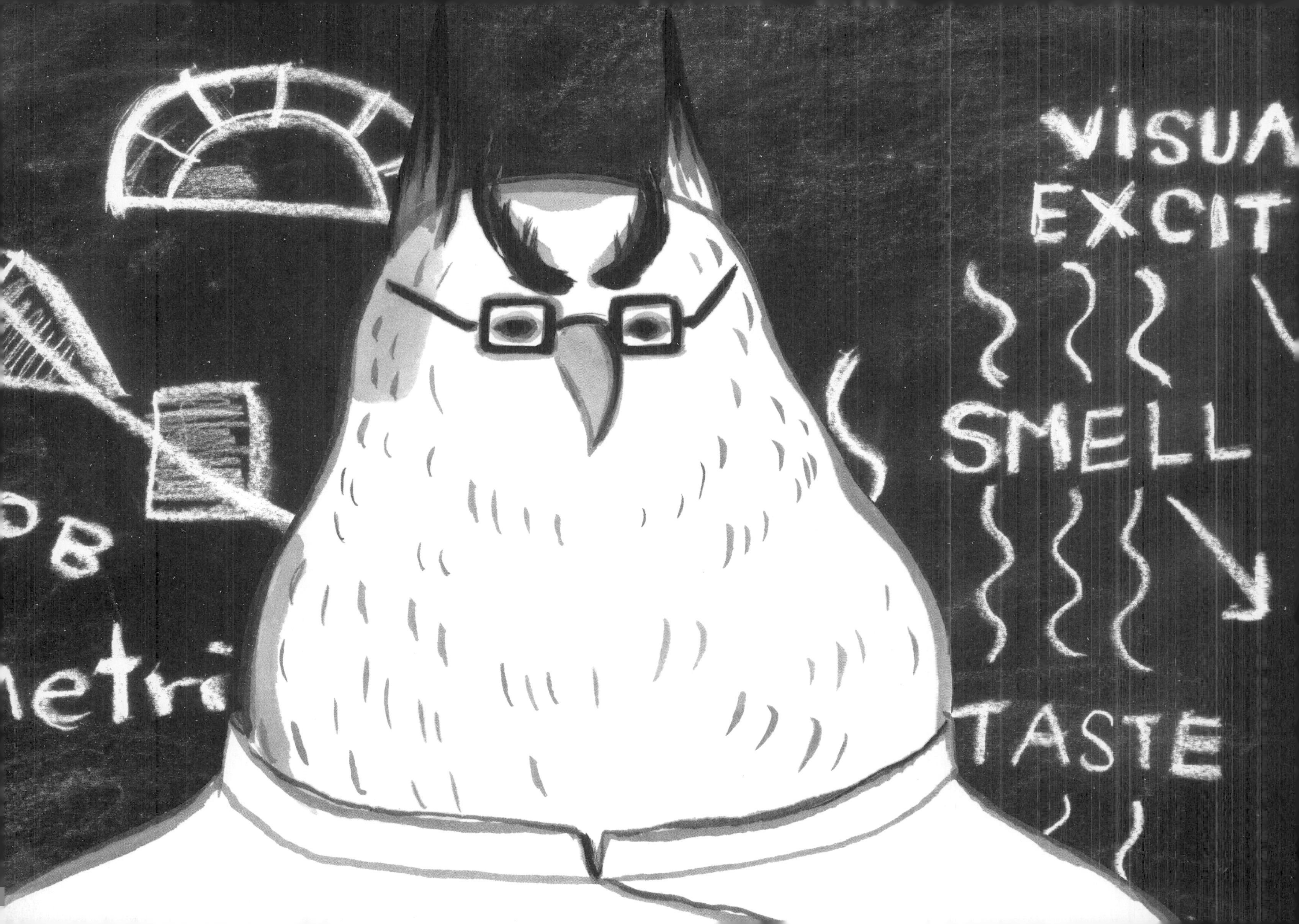

VISUA
EXCIT
SMELL
TASTE
DB
metri

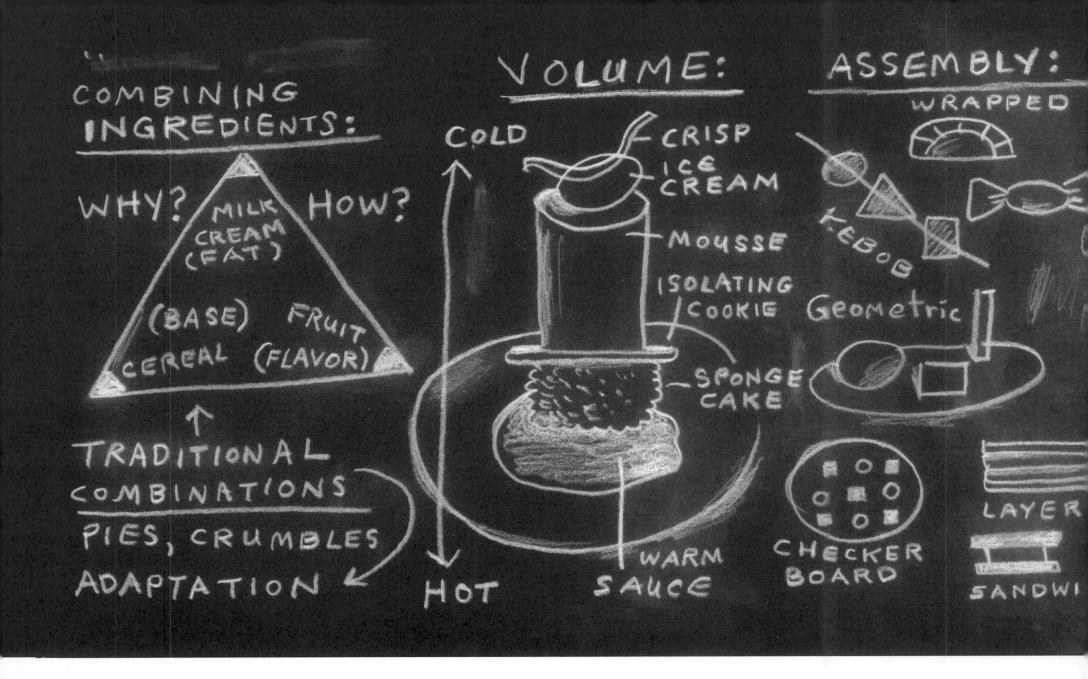

"See how easy it is? Questions, anyone?"

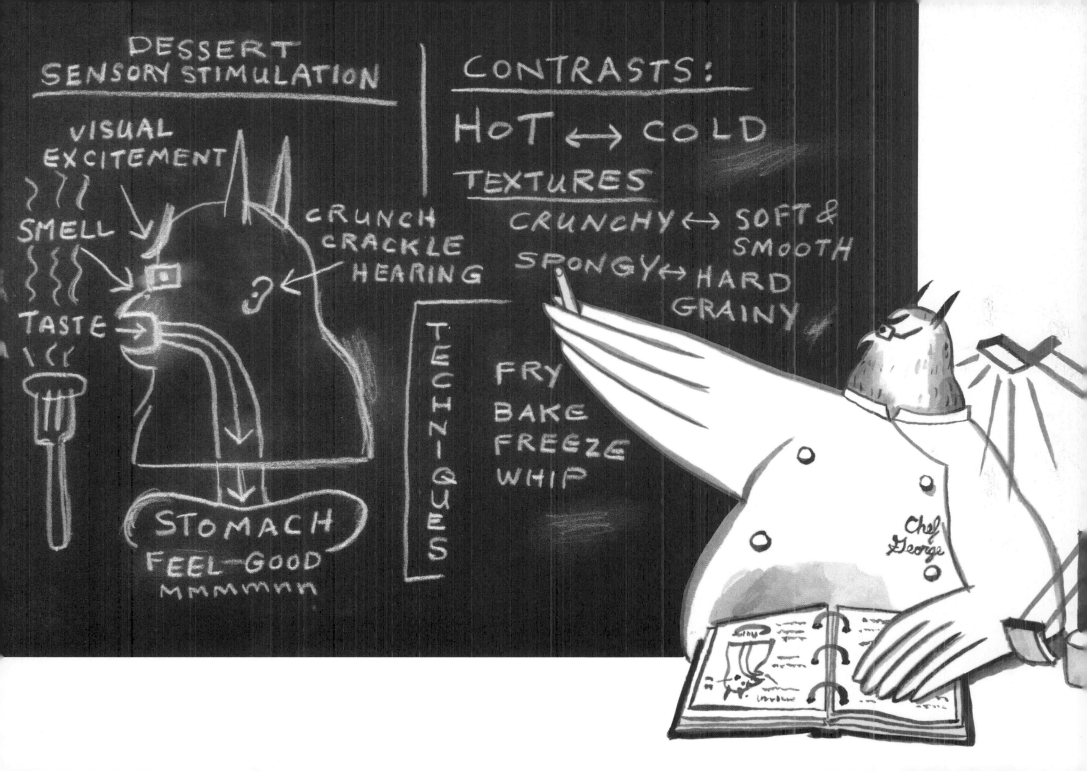

"Looks like we're going to have to start at the beginning.

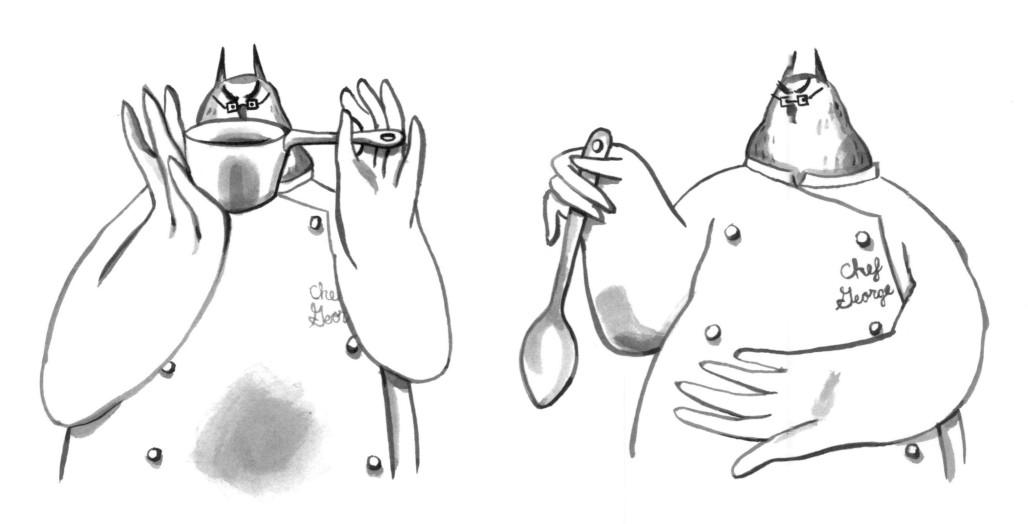

This is a pot.

This is a spoon.

This is an egg . . .

. . . and this is a pot on a stove."

"And these are a few recipes from the world's greatest dessert chef."

SUBLIME SHORTCAKE CHEF GEORGE

C.G.'s Fanciful Fondues

CHEF GEORGE'S SENSIBLE SWEETS

Chef George's Perfect Pies

C.G's Impeccable Pastries

FABULOUS FUDGE by Chef George

C.G.'s INCREDIBLE ICE CREAM

Chef George's Festive Finger Foods

...g Buns...George

"Now the time has come to train your noses.

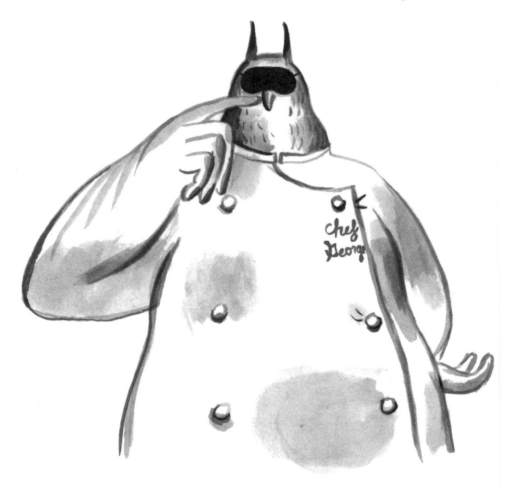

Cover your eyes and tell me what
you smell. And no, no, no peeking!"

After many hours of instruction, the moment to start baking has finally arrived. "On your marks, get set, GO!"

"Take the time to measure carefully."

"Sometimes teamwork is necessary . . .

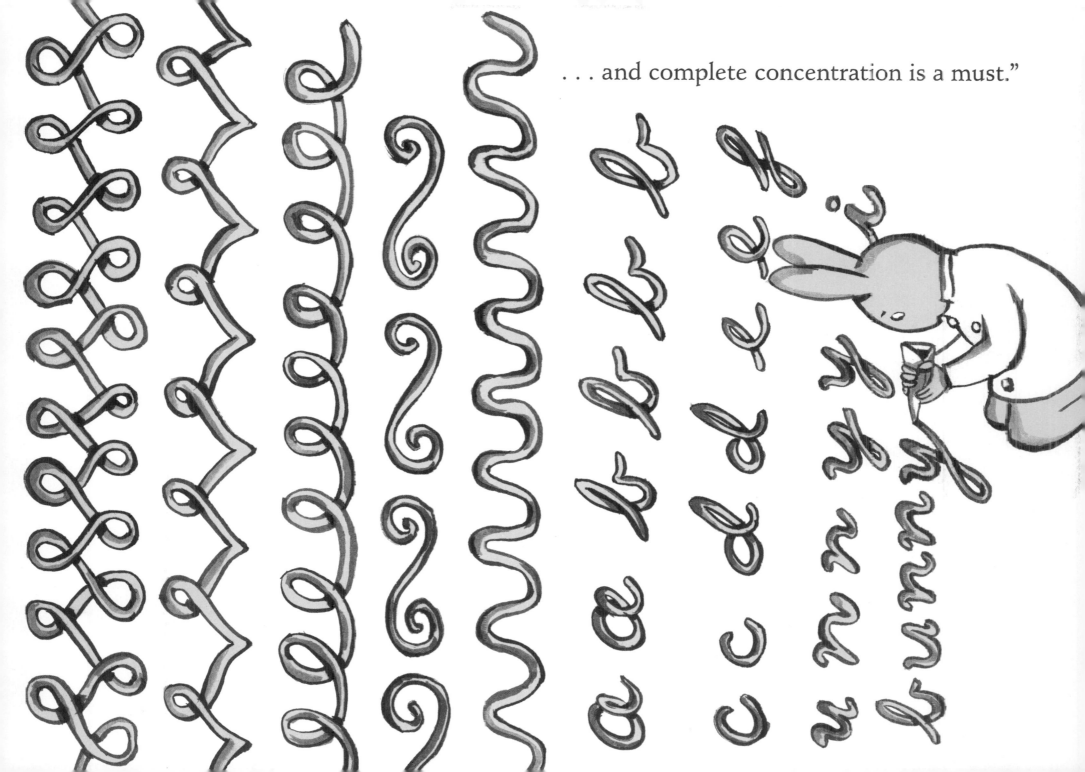

. . . and complete concentration is a must."

"A dessert should smell as good as it tastes."

"The kitchen must be kept neat and orderly . . ."

Ta-da!
Finished!
Would anybody
like a bite?

"Fine job, everyone! Now line up with the rest
of your desserts, and smile for the camera."

C.G.'S CRAZY COCONUT LIME MACAROONS

4 cups grated unsweetened coconut
1 cup ground almonds
zest of 1-1/2 limes
2 tablespoons confectioner's sugar
3 large egg whites
1/2 cup granulated sugar

Have ready:
2 cookie sheets lined with parchment paper

Preheat the oven to 300° F. Mix together the coconut, almonds, lime zest, and confectioner's sugar.

Beat the egg whites with the granulated sugar until stiff peaks form. Using a spatula, mix the dry ingredients with the egg whites. Drop large teaspoonfuls 2 inches apart onto the prepared cookie sheets. Bake for about 15 minutes, or until lightly browned. Let cool on the baking sheets. Makes about 3 dozen. Irresistible!

C.G.'S CRUNCHY RICE PISTACHIO BRICKS

5 cups crisped rice cereal
1 cup shelled pistachios
1/4 cup unsalted butter
4 cups small marshmallows

Have ready:
an 8x8-inch cake pan, greased
a large wooden spoon

Mix the rice cereal and pistachios in a bowl and set aside. In a large pot, melt the butter. Add the marshmallows, stirring constantly until melted. Remove from the heat. Add the cereal mixture and stir until it's completely coated. Pour into the pan and press with the back of a wooden spoon.

Cool completely. Cut into rectangles. Makes 2 dozen bricks. Bet you can't eat just one!